Fly Away!

by Dana Catharine
illustrated by Bill Ogden

Printed in the United States of America

ISBN 0-15-317210-X – Fly Away

Ordering Options
ISBN 0-15-318597-X (Package of 5)
ISBN 0-15-316985-0 (Grade 1 Package)

2 3 4 5 6 7 8 9 10 179 02 01 00

I put up a bird feeder outside
my room. I like to feed the
birds. They eat the seeds I put
out. They sing to me.

Last spring, two birds flew right up to my feeder. They began making a little nest.

2

I watched the birds every
day. I wanted to learn how they
made their nest. They were
using sticks, dirt, and leaves.

One day, I saw three eggs in the nest. The mama bird sat on the eggs. She sat there day after day. Sometimes she moved the eggs around a little.

4

Then one day, I saw three
baby birds in the nest! They
were very small. I could hear
them chirping. I thought that
they might want some food.

I watched as the small birds
grew and grew. They sat on the
side of the nest and looked out.
They held on tight and flapped
their wings.

6

Soon it was time for the baby birds to learn to fly. One baby bird flew out of the nest. It was a short flight!

The nest was so high! The
other two babies were afraid
they'd fall but they tried to fly.
Soon, they flew down to the
grass. They joined the other
baby bird.

All day, the baby birds
tried to fly. The mama and
papa birds watched. That night,
the baby birds flew into the
roses.

Soon all three little birds
were flying high in the bright
sunlight. They loved flying!

10

I have a bright red bike.
At first, I wouldn't ride it.
I was afraid I might fall. Then I
thought about the baby birds.
They were not afraid to fly.

"Will you help me learn to ride my bike?" I asked my mom and dad. Then, just like the baby birds, I tried and tried. Now, look at me. I'm riding!

12

Teacher/Family Member ....

I Think I Can!
Ask children to share things that were difficult for them to learn.
Encourage them to tell how they felt when they tried the activity for
the first time.

 School-Home Connection
Invite your child to read *Fly Away!* to you. Ask your child how the girl
helped the birds. Then ask how the birds helped the girl.

Word Count: 306

Vocabulary Words:
flew
learn
afraid
joined

Phonic Elements:
Long Vowel: /ī/*igh*

high	bright
right	might
flight	tight
sunlight	night

Inflections: *-ed, -ing* (drop final e)

making	using
moved	loved
riding	

....

TAKE-HOME BOOK
Set Sail
Use with "The Story of a Blue Bird."